THE
ARRANGEMENT
VOL. 5

H.M. Ward

www.SexyAwesomeBooks.com

Laree Bailey Press

This book is a work of fiction. Names, characters, places, and
incidents are either the product of the author's imagination or are
used fictitiously, and any resemblance to actual persons, living or
dead, events, or locales is entirely coincidental.

ISBN: 978-0615827834
Laree Bailey Press
First Print Edition: May 2013

THE ARRANGEMENT

VOL. 5

CHAPTER 1

Strange dreams plague me. Memories are tangled up in older memories. Everything is so convoluted that I don't know what's real. Time no longer exists. I can't feel my head, although I know it was throbbing a few moments ago. To make things stranger, my parents are talking to me. They tell me it's all right. They look exactly the same way they did the last time I saw them. My mom has her gold cross around her neck. The light catches it, and it grows brighter.

The scene shifts. There's no floor or walls. Only darkness. I blink over and over again, trying to focus on something. My skin prickles as if someone is looking at me. When my eyes adjust, I can see the outline of a familiar form. He comes into focus. Sean's blue gaze meets mine from across the room. My heart thumps hard. I want to walk to him, but my feet won't move. Sean says nothing. He stands there like a ghost, flickering in and out of focus. The haunted expression I've seen so many times is still etched onto his face. It's like there are things that he wants to say, but he doesn't move. He doesn't try to come to me.

I don't know how long it lasts. It feels painful. Neither of us can move. There are so many things to say, but neither of us speaks. The silence is deafening. Then he walks toward me.

Sean's voice is a whisper of music. It's too soft to be heard, but I hear it. His hand strokes my cheek and soothing words fall from his lips. *I love you, Avery. I'm so sorry I never told you.*

Sean's touch lingers, and then he slowly steps away. The inky blackness engulfs him and I'm alone. Time passes slowly, and nothing happens for a long time.

Then, my body grows colder. Sweat drips down my spine and soaks my hair. A bead trickles down my cheek and I wipe it away. I try to suck in air, but find I can't breathe. I panic. The floor is gone and I'm falling, suddenly sucked into a black hole. I'm breathless. My stomach flies up into my throat and I flail, trying to grab hold of something. My mouth is open. I scream, and hear an echo that sounds too far away.

Suddenly, I feel my arms and legs. Sheets are tangling me. Panic has me in an icy sweat. I push up before my eyes are open, gasping.

"Whoa," a male voice says. His hand is on my shoulder, steadying me. My head throbs and the room spins. The hand pushes me back down. I freak out and yelp.

"Damn, Avery. You're all sorts of messed up. Stay still. It's just Marty and me. What the hell did they give you?" Mel is talking. I can't focus on her face.

I stretch my fingers and feel the IV in my hand. The tape itches. My eyes feel like they're stitched together. I manage to pry them open and look around. The room is spinning. I groan and cover my face with my hands, trying to make it stop. When I lay still, things settle. I feel like I'm drugged out of my mind. I wonder if Marty and Mel are real or if I'm still dreaming. I look straight ahead. Mel is at the foot of my bed. I sweep my eyes across the room. Marty is next to me in a chair. I'm not in the same room I fell asleep in.

My brain wakes up and shakes off. Panic is prodding it to function faster and piece things together. Frantic thoughts fly through my mind like an out of control kaleidoscope.

They admitted me? I can't be here. I can't afford this. Anxiety rises up from deep inside me and vines into every crevice of my being. If I can't pay these bills, I'll have to declare bankruptcy. If I declare bankruptcy, then I can't get a job when I graduate, which means my entire life is a wash. Everything I did to stay in college will be wiped out.

I completely freak out. My heart is pounding as though someone is trying to kill me. My voice sounds like a screech, "I can't be here. I can't—" I start coughing and can't stop. My mouth and throat are so dry. My lips are bloody and cracked in the corners. I'd kill someone for Blistex right now.

"Shhh, Avery. Everything will be fine," Marty says, and hands me a cup of water. I take it, grateful, and sip. I keep clearing my throat, trying to swallow. After a moment, he asks, "Better?"

I nod and hand him back the cup. My hands shake. There's another question that I've been dreading to ask, but I need to know. The dream has me spooked. Sean shouldn't be standing by my parents, not unless he's dead. I want to curl into a ball and cry.

I manage, "Where is Sean?" Mel looks at Marty, but neither of them says anything. "Tell me. If he's d-dead, tell me. I can't take not knowing. Where is he?"

Marty looks down at me. His fingers stroke my forehead gently. "We're not sure. They moved you up here last night. Mel and I got here right after they moved you. I heard they were working on a guy that was in a motorcycle accident when we came in through the ER. I'm guessing that was Sean, but no one will tell us anything.

"Mel grabbed your chart when nobody was looking and wrote down that she was your next of kin, otherwise they wouldn't have even let us in to see you."

Mel snorts. "Yeah, they didn't believe we were sisters. I told them if they wanted to hear the fucked up shit we've been through, I got time. They let me in after that and I brought Marty up. I think I scared that little blonde nurse you had last night."

Marty laughs. "Yeah, she thinks we're in a gang or something."

"A gay gang. That'll do wonders for my reputation." Mel sits down on a chair and looks so sullen, so sorry. She blinks away all her sass and for a moment, she's nothing but worried. "Seriously, Avery, are you all right? Do you hurt? You want more pain meds?"

I shake my head slowly. "No, I don't think so. Whatever they gave to me, made me feel weird. So, what's wrong with me? Why was I admitted? I have no insurance. I can't possibly pay for this." My heart starts pounding again.

Marty sits back in his chair. He presses his fingers together. "I think you're here under observation. They said you hit your head pretty hard. They ran a bunch of tests last night and are still waiting on some of the results. Don't worry. They'll throw your ass out as soon as possible."

Mel sighs and says, "Black was here. Gabe or Blade or whatever the hell his name is, is in the waiting room to see if you wake up."

"Black came? Who told her?" Damn, my head hurts. I rub my fingers against my temples, squinting, trying to focus.

"I did," Mel says. "You were wearing your bracelet. The bead broke and she called you. Her thug showed up two seconds later to skin your date, but I told him what happened. Black wants her investment back."

"Shit." I close my eyes. I think about it for a moment, and then ask. "Is Sean's jacket in here?" Mel nods and hands it to me. I pull out the envelope and separate the note, the necklace, and some of the money. I put those things back in Sean's jacket and hand it back to Mel. "Call Gabe in here for me."

"Avery—" Marty interrupts. He cuts Mel a look that says she shouldn't listen to me, but Mel does. Before he can protest, Mel is in the hallway. "You don't have to do this now." His eyes are so big and brown. I never realized how much he cares about me. Marty looks really worried.

I take his hand and rub the back. "It'll be okay. Wait and see."

Gabe walks in. "Miss Stanz, how are you?"

"I've been better. Listen, I know why you're here. Take this. Give it to Black. Tell her we're even. I took out enough to cover the fee from the other night." I hand him the envelope filled with cash. "Tell her my indentured servitude is over."

He looks down at it and back up at me. "I'll let her know. What about work? Should I tell her you're coming back? Or are you making other employment arrangements?"

I want to quit. Since I stepped my foot into Black's office, things have gone from bad to worse. But I can't pull out. Not now. God knows how much this is going to cost. I'll have to pay the debt, and finish school and work. Oh, holy hell. My head hurts. I'm staring at Gabe as I'm thinking. The answer is obvious. I have to keep working for her. Shit.

"Avery…" Marty says softly.

Mel watches me, her caramel eyes flicking between me and Gabe.

"I'll come back as soon as possible. I want to be on the books next weekend. I'm full in, none of this halfway stuff anymore."

Gabe nods, "You're made of stone, kid. Hold it together and get out as fast as you can." Gabe glances at Mel and adds, "I never said that, so you didn't hear it."

Mel flinches and looks at me, and then back at Gabe. "I'm not saying shit to no one. What you looking at me like that for? The more people looking out for my girl, the better. Damn right, I said that. Tell whoever the fuck you want." Mel's arms are folded over her chest. Standing next to Gabe, she looks so small and breakable.

Gabe smirks at Mel and leaves without another word. We all watch the door close. I rub the heel of my hand over my eyes and sit up. The room tilts to the side, but I can't stay here. I have to get up and leave. Before I can manage to swing my legs off the side of the bed, Marty scoots closer and takes my hand.

"Avery, how could you say that?" Marty sounds like he's scolding me.

"Don't you dare yell at her. What the hell is wrong with you? She's been through enough. Zip it, Dough Boy or I'll toss your ass out of here." Mel is standing with her hands on her hips. I can tell that she wants to yell at Marty, but her voice is calm.

She looks over at me. "You hungry? I'll go get you something, some soup maybe? I know how much you like soup."

I like soup as much as she likes pancakes. I smile. It makes my lips crack. I wince and ask, "Sounds good. And can you find me some lip balm?"

Mel nods. "Sure thing, honey. Glad you're alive."

"Me too."

Mel slips out the door, and Marty and I are alone.

CHAPTER 2

Marty doesn't say anything, at first. He seems nervous and way out of sorts. I tell him, "I don't think anything is broken. I can move all my toes."

"Avery, I need to tell you something. After all this, oh my God, if I didn't get a chance to say it…"

I smile at him. My face hurts to do it, but he looks so scared. "Just tell me."

"The other day when I broke the beaker… Do you remember?"

Yeah, I remember. He was acting like a crazy person. I nod. "Yeah, what was that about?"

Marty watches me for a long time. There's no expression on his face. I sigh and rub my shoulder. It feels like the muscles have a rock stuck between them. Marty leans forward and says, "Here, let me help." His hands work my shoulder and I can feel the muscle start to loosen up.

"So, about the other day?" I prompt.

"Yeah, the thing is—damn, I don't even know where to start. Sometimes things don't work out the way you think, you know? You go into a situation thinking one thing, but then everything changes, and nothing goes the way you planned." Marty's hands work my shoulder, rubbing out the sore muscles. I relax a little.

"You're preaching to choir."

"Yeah, well, there's more." He rubs his thumb into the muscle harder, and I make a content sound, a gentle moan. Marty jerks his hand away like I burned him. I glance at him, not understanding. "Avery, I—"

There's a knock at the door, cutting him off. A man in scrubs and a white lab coat enters. "Avery Stanz, good to see you awake. How do you feel?"

"Like I was in a car wreck. Sore and achy."

He nods and looks at my clipboard. "Any vision issues? Difficulty walking? Headaches?"

My head hurts, but I want to leave. I say no to all three, even though I haven't been out of bed. He asks me more questions and explains that my tests came back clear and that I can go home. They held me here because I had an allergic reaction to a pain killer they gave me in the ER. He explains what drug it was and tells me that I need to remember it. Apparently, I was hallucinating and had trouble breathing right. They pumped me full of an antihistamine and kept me longer to be safe.

Just before the doctor walks away, he asks, "Any questions?"

I nod and look up at him. "Where is Sean Ferro? No one will tell me anything."

He smiles sadly. "Your friend is...something. He, uh," the doctor glances back at the door and then back at me. "He's no longer with us. He—"

I gasp and my hands fly to my face. The doctor keeps talking, but I've shut him out. I hear his voice but not his words. It isn't until I feel his hand on my shoulder that I can focus enough to hear what he's saying. "Miss Stanz, please listen. Your friend signed himself out last night. I said that poorly. I didn't mean to frighten you. Mr. Ferro is banged up, but he'll recover. Do you understand?"

Eyes wide, I nod. "Sean's alive?"

"Yes, he is." The doctor releases my shoulder. His gaze cuts to Marty. "Make sure she remembers what I said." And then to me, "The nurse will be by to discharge you in a little bit. I ah, heard something last night. Is it true that Mr. Ferro cut off your car to avoid that truck?" he asks, looking directly at me. I nod. My throat is too tight to speak.

He studies me for a moment and points his pen at me. "You're very fortunate. You both are. The paramedics showed me pictures of his bike. Luck was on your side." He shakes his head, like he can't believe it, and leaves.

I laugh. I can't help it. I'm the antithesis of lucky. "No, I'm not. Luck evades me."

"Not this time, Avery." Marty pats my arm. "You were damn lucky. So was Sean." Marty blinks, like that's the craziest thing he's ever heard. "I can't believe he walked out."

Neither can I. He walked out and left me here. Sean didn't wait for me. He didn't make sure I was okay, he just left. Who does that? The floor of my stomach twists with worry.

CHAPTER 3

Marty and Mel work out who will take me home. The doctor said that someone needs to keep an eye on me. I agreed to let them, but now that I'm being buckled into Marty's front seat I no longer want to cooperate. I want to see Sean. I need to look at him with my own eyes and see that he's alive. I don't understand how he could fall like that and walk away. I don't understand. It seems unreal, like everything else in my life.

Marty is driving toward the college. He's talking softly, asking me if I'm okay, if

I want food or something. I stare out the window. There's something cold inside my stomach and it's creeping up my throat. I don't know what happened, but I feel like I can't tell him what I'm thinking, not after this.

Marty's big brown eyes cut over to me. I feel them on the side of my face, poking me like a stick. "Tell me what crazy idea is brewing in that head of yours."

I look at him with my jaw hanging open. Damn it. How does he do that? Why am I so transparent around him? I try to throw him off. "What? I wouldn't—"

"Cut the crap, princess. I see that look on your face. What crazy-ass thing are you planning this time?"

I sink down into my seat and fold my arms across my chest. Marty slows the car as we hit gridlock. Awesome. "You make me sound like a Scooby-Doo villain. I'm not planning anything."

"As soon as I tuck you into your little bed and chase Amber away, you're going to go to him. Am I right?" Marty gives me a look.

My gaze drops to my hands. I feel like crap. I'm exhausted in every way possible. My voice is weak and mousy, hardly audible. "I need to see him."

"That guy has brought you nothing but trouble. I'm all for true love and fighting for what you believe in, but this isn't love Avery. Don't make me tell you what it is. You already know." Marty's grip tightens on the steering wheel. The car inches forward. A horn blares somewhere behind us.

"I have to see him," I repeat. "I don't expect you to understand, but after everything I've been through—I have to see him. I can't believe he walked away from that, like I literally cannot believe it. I have to see for myself... and I need to ask him something."

Marty is silent for a moment. He works his jaw while staring straight ahead. Suddenly, his eyes cut to the left and then back to the right. He mutters something that I can't make out and edges the car into the far left lane. "Mel is going to kill me. I swear to God, if you tell her that I—"

I realize that he's turning around, that Marty is going to take me back to the city so I can see Sean. "Thank you, Marty. Really, I—"

He shakes his head and gives me a firm look. "Don't thank me. This is the worst possible thing I could do for you." His eyes bore into me, which makes me squirm in my seat. There's something there, some grievance or grief that I'm unaware of—something I don't know. I want to ask why he's so bent on keeping me away from Sean, but I know better than to ask.

The light changes and Marty does a U-turn and we're out of gridlock, heading directly toward Sean's hotel. I tell Marty where to go and then there's a thick uncomfortable silence.

My finger flicks the leather on the door as I stare out the window. My mind keeps drifting back to the note in Sean's pocket. He regrets everything. He wants to start over. In that moment, I feel the same way. I want to throw my arms around his neck and kiss him until I can't breathe, but how can I —he left without me. Sean didn't even make sure I was all right. He didn't stick his head in and check on me. He did nothing. It looks like he doesn't care about me at all.

I groan and rub my face with the heel of my hand. My head is pounding. I glance over at Marty. "You think I'm making a mistake, don't you?"

Marty glances over at me before his eyes dart back to the road. "Don't ask me questions that you already know the answer to," he snaps. He's so tense. It's like he's strangling the steering wheel as he drives. When we are approaching the hotel, he finally speaks. "I'm parking and walking up with you."

"Marty—"

"It's not optional. Besides, you look like you're going to do a face-plant on the dashboard. I can't let you wander in by yourself." Marty pulls up in front of the hotel and gives his car to the valet.

When I step out, the guy that opened my door gives me a weird look. I have that train wreck thing going on. I haven't even looked in a mirror. Who cares about mirrors at times like this? But still, it makes me feel self-conscious. Marty hands him a fist full of cash and takes my arm. I hold onto Marty. I am weak. The world starts to tilt to the side, but Marty steadies me and the feeling passes.

As we walk inside, Marty leans in and whispers in my ear, "You owe me so big for this, and I totally plan on redeeming this time." His palm rubs the back of my hand and he grins at me.

My heart is pounding. My thoughts tangle tighter and tighter as the elevator approaches Sean's floor. I try to swallow the lump in my throat, but it won't move. Marty squeezes my hand tight and says, "You okay?"

I nod and smile at him. Worry pinches my face though, so the smile looks timid. The elevator doors open. I turn to Marty and ask, "Will you wait for me over here?"

"Avery, I don't think you should see him alone. This is a really bad idea. The guy left—he left you in the hospital alone." Marty is pleading with me, but I can't bend to caution. I have to see for myself.

I pat his hands before saying, "Thank you," and turning away. I walk slowly toward Sean's door.

Every inch of my body aches. It doesn't matter that I have a ton of pain killers in me. When my foot hits the floor, it feels like nails are being jammed into my joints. I lift my hand to knock, but hesitate.

What am I doing here? What is it that I want from this man? He's messed up beyond comprehension, and for some reason I'm standing on his doorstep. My hand lingers by the door. Thinking swiftly, I decide that I just want to see Sean. I need to know that he's alive. My knuckles wrap against the wood twice and then I drop my hand to my side.

When the door is pulled open, my heart drops into my shoes. Sean is standing there bleary-eyed. His shirt is open, revealing some nasty bruises on his skin. "Avery," he breathes my name, surprised to see me. "What are you doing here?"

My lips part to say something, but I can't speak. Marty walks up behind me and produces Sean's jacket. "She wanted to bring you back your stuff. The hospital gave it to her." I smile at Marty, grateful. I don't know where my courage went, but it's gone. I don't like the look in Sean's eye. I take

Sean's jacket and remove the envelope before handing him the beat up leather.

Sean stares at Marty with venom in his eyes, before his gaze shifts back to me. Sean takes the jacket and says, "Come in." I nod and walk past him, into the hotel room. Marty remains in the hall way, but Sean doesn't leave it alone. "You too, get in here."

Marty tenses. He gives me a look that lets me know that he really can't stand Sean. The door closes behind us and Marty crosses the room to look out a window. I know he's trying to give me space, but Sean's watching Marty like he's a threat.

I step toward Sean, saying, "How are you all right? After you fell, you didn't move. I couldn't feel you breathing." My eyes are as big as saucers and they start to burn. The expression Sean gives me is unreadable, cold.

"I wasn't. The wind got knocked out of me when I fell. I couldn't say anything. The helmet and jacket saved my skin. It's armored. I have a gash on my leg where my jeans got shredded, but the rest of me is fine." Sean's lips barely move when he says *fine*. It's like he's saying that he's anything but fine.

I nod. My pulse is pounding in my ears and my skin is prickling with sweat. I lift the letter between my fingers. Dread fills me, making it difficult to breathe. "I found this in your things."

He stares at me. "And you read it?"

I nod. "I didn't know what happened to you. When I saw my name on the envelope, I..." my voice trails off. What am I doing here? Sean obviously doesn't want to see me.

"Did you give the money to Black?"

"Yeah, I did." Sean nods slowly. His eyes keep flicking up toward the spot where Marty is standing, looking out the window. I hold up the letter again. Sean looks at the paper and then at me. "What about this?"

"What about it?" Sean holds my gaze. He almost seems defiant and I don't understand why. After a moment, he turns away. His face pinches slightly and he has a slight limp when he steps away from me.

Anger flashes through my veins. A million thoughts collide inside my mind and explode out my mouth. "*What about it?* Oh,

I don't know. Was it true? Did you just write it so we're even and you could give me back the money I threw in your face? Or was it something else?" I want to scream at him, but I don't. Instead, I take a slow breath in and when I look up from under my brow, I catch his eyes. "Tell me the truth. How do you feel about me? Man up and say it, instead of cowering behind silence."

Marty has turned. I can feel his eyes on my back, but he remains by the window.

Sean seems so detached, like he doesn't care about me one way or the other. "Actions speak louder than words, don't they? Add it up, Avery."

I know what he's saying. Sean is denying he has any feelings for me at all. "Bullshit. You're a coward. Your actions ring so goddamn loud that they're constantly gonging in my head. You threw yourself under a truck for me. Then, you ditched me. You stormed out the hospital without even checking on me!"

I shove his chest because Sean is no longer meeting my gaze. His face is turned to the side, like I've slapped his cheek. My heart feels hollowed out. Why won't he tell me? Desperation fills me like a storm. It violently tears away all rational thought until I'm close to tears.

Sean runs his hand through his dark hair and looks over his shoulder at Marty. "Take her home. Play house. Do whatever it is that you two do." Sean walks toward the door and holds it open.

My jaw drops. I glance back at Marty who is giving Sean the nastiest look I've ever seen. When I glance at Sean, I see it. He thinks Marty and I are an item. I step in front of Sean and tug his shirtfront hard, pulling his face closer to mine. "Marty's a friend, you idiot, and right now he's a better friend than you are." I shove past Sean to walk out the door, but he catches my hand. I look back at him, ready to bite his head off, but the expression on his face stops me.

"Wait…" Sean's voice trails off as he looks away.

Marty is behind me. I know he wants to leave, but my feet freeze. The plea in Sean's voice holds me in place. His fingers are wrapped around my wrist, which makes my stomach do summersaults. My spine stiffens.

I try to push the sensations away. I'm tired of playing games. I don't know what I expected of Sean, but this isn't it. "No, I'm done with this. You can't even tell me why you left. Your frickin' leg is bleeding through your jeans. You left the hospital without even letting them patch you up. You left me behind. I can't do this anymore. I'm done." I'm so weary. I just want to leave. My mistakes are crushing me. Coming here was a mistake. I shake my head and try to pull away, but Sean doesn't let go.

Something changes. I sense it and look up at him. "I'll tell you. Stay and I'll tell you." Sean's eyes meet mine and I feel my resolve flake off and blow away.

I glance at Marty. He rolls his eyes and heads out the door. Before leaving he turns back to me. "Some things are beyond your control, Avery, but other things—" Marty shakes his head, "other heartache is completely preventable." Marty narrows his eyes at Sean, in a hateful glare, waits half a beat, and leaves.

Dread runs down my spine. Why does it feel like I just made a huge mistake?

CHAPTER 4

When the door closes, Sean seems stiff. I wonder if he aches as much as I do. I wonder if it feels like his heart has been ripped out of his chest one too many times. I don't understand him. I don't know why he keeps running hot and cold. I have emotional whiplash and I'm too tired to deal with it.

When Sean doesn't say anything, I move to the door and reach out for the handle. "Listen, my ride is leaving and I'm too tired for this. If you don't—"

Sean makes an exasperated sound and drags his palms over his face. "What, you think I can just come out and say it?"

Looking over my shoulder, I answer, "Yeah. Say something or I'm gone."

For a moment I'm nervous that Sean won't tell me, that he'll let me leave. I don't want things to end like this, but he has to at least try to talk to me. I can't take living this way anymore. I'm in love with him and it kills me that I can't even tell if he likes me. I let out an annoyed sound and yank open the door.

Just as I'm about to walk through, Sean speaks. "I don't like hospitals. They upset me. A lot. I ran out before they could work on me, but I did see you. I came into your room."

Turning slowly, I look at him. Sean's shoulders are slumped, his jaw is covered in day-old scruff, and he isn't looking at me. My hand rests on the handle. "I don't remember seeing you. I thought you were dead." The last sentence is barely a whisper.

Anxiety that I didn't have time to deal with before rears its head and I feel unstable. I want to yell, scream, and cry. I want to bang my fists into his chest and have him pull me into his arms and tell me that everything will be all right, but I can't break down like that. I don't have the luxury.

Sean's lips part. He breathes for a moment, like it pains him. When his blue gaze meets mine, I know he's lost in his past. I recognize the look in his eye. I've seen it in the mirror too many times to count. He runs his hand through his hair and down his neck. "You were sedated when I found you. I would have taken you with me, but your *friend* chased me off." Sean's eyes dart to the open door.

"Marty?"

He nods. "It's none of my business what you do with your life, but that guy wants you." Sean slips his hands into his pockets.

My jaw drops. I make some strangled sounds before sputtering out, "He's gay! Marty's gay! You are so far off base that you don't even know what you're talking about." I want to laugh because it seems insane, but I don't. Sean's serious.

He shrugs. "It doesn't matter. That look is still there. The way he ran me off spoke volumes."

"You're wrong. Marty's as into me sexually as Mel is. There's nothing between me and either one of them, so stop making excuses. Why'd you run?"

Sean sighs and looks up at the ceiling. After a second, he says, "Close the door. I'll have a car take you home when you want to leave." I don't like the way he's talking to me, but I let the door shut and step into the room. I fold my arms over my chest and wait.

Sean doesn't look at me when he speaks. "Hospitals give me a great deal of anxiety."

"That's not an answer."

Sean glances up at me. His eyes are cold and hard. They could cut through metal. I flinch. "Let me finish. I won't say it twice." I swallow hard and sit down on a chair next to the table by the door. Sean paces as he talks. There's a slight limp when he steps. His hands remain in his pockets.

He stares straight ahead, not looking at me. "It's not hospitals in general, it's *that* hospital. That's where I lost them. Being in the same place, standing in the same rooms, was too much. I'd rather leave and die on the sidewalk than stay in that place." Each word is loaded with emotion, pulled from the depths of his soul.

I don't know what to say. I want to make him feel better, but nothing I say will remove the memory from his mind.

And now I know what happened to the baby. He said *them*. He must have lost his wife and baby at the same time. I press my lips together tightly. No wonder why he's emotionally repressed. Losing one person is hard enough, but losing two is an unfathomable amount of pain. My parents' deaths were hard enough. I can't image losing a spouse and a child.

When Sean looks up at me, I can't hide the pity in my eyes. "Don't look at me like that. You don't understand what happened."

"Then tell me."

He laughs. It sounds so bitter and broken. I know he feels hollowed out inside. I feel the same way. His words are sharp. "If baring my soul was cathartic, I would have done it already."

I fold my hands in my lap. "Then maybe you're doing it wrong."

Sean gives me a look. "Reliving the past doesn't change the present."

"It made you who you are. And it would sure as hell help me figure out what the hell is going on inside your head."

He smirks. "You really don't want to go in there."

"How could you throw yourself in front of a truck for me, and then leave? I know you said Marty tossed you out, but Sean…" As I speak, he steps closer and closer to my chair. The look in his eyes changes from defensive to something that makes my skin tingle. My stomach tightens. Sean stops in front of me. He looks down at my hands. He takes one and threads our fingers together before lowering himself to his knees.

Sean looks at our fingers. "You don't want to know everything. Trust me."

"How can I, when you act like this? I don't know why—" He rubs the back of my hand with his thumbs. His eyes are locked with mine. I want to throw myself into his arms so badly.

"This is who I am. I'm not a good catch, Avery. I'm fucked up. You know that. You know me well enough to see it. I don't pretend to be something I'm not. No amount of talking will fix anything I've done. No amount of explaining will justify my choices. There's no reason for you to be here. There's nothing left that's worth saving." Sean buries his face in my lap and holds onto me like he's drowning and I'm the only one who can save him.

Bleary-eyed, I stare straight ahead with my mouth hanging open. Words won't come. I run my fingers through his hair, gently. I rub my hands over his shoulders and neck, wishing that I could ease some of his pain. We sit like that. It feels like half the night passes before he looks up at me.

When he finally does, Sean stands and takes my hand. He pulls me to my feet and over to the bed. We crawl under the covers and hold each other until sleep finally comes.

CHAPTER 5

I wake up the next morning with a bitching headache. I stretch and instantly regret it. I blink a few times and remember where I am. There's an arm across my middle. I smile and look over at Sean. He's awake, watching me.

"I'm not letting you go," he says. There are bruises on his face, but most are under the stubble.

I smile. "Then give me a reason to stay." I roll onto my side and Sean pulls us together. My heart pounds harder. I can feel every curve of his ripped body against me.

Sean lowers his head and presses his lips to my neck. I shiver and hold my breath. "I shouldn't." He kisses my neck again. His lips slip over my skin, and his tongue evokes a slew of sensations that shoot through my body.

"Sean," I moan his name and push him away. "We can't…"

But Sean doesn't stay away. Instead, he comes on stronger with delicious, delicate touches that make me close my eyes and beg for more. Then, he abruptly stops. "Alright, we can stop." He's grinning at me. Sean's made me all hot and bothered and then stopped.

I shove him and laugh, "You suck."

"I tried, but you said no." He gives me a crooked grin and sits up. He still has that rumpled shirt on with the front hanging open. Sean kicks the covers off and stands.

"How's your leg?"

"Better. Everything is better today." Sean turns back to the bed and says, "Pretend with me for a while?" He holds out his hand for me, but I don't take it.

"What do you mean?"

"We can't have a relationship because of your job and because of—well, me and my preferences—but we can pretend for a moment, for a shower, that we're normal people. I can help you get dressed. Help you scrub off in the shower, you know, normal things that normal people do." Sean looks hopeful. His voice is so soft and sweet.

"You want me to take a shower with you?" He nods. "Because it's not a violation of Black's contract and because it's not that weird kind of sex you like?"

He pulls me to his feet. "Because we're both dirty and need to get dressed. Stop overthinking it. If the idea of rubbing soap over my stomach appeals to you, then follow me. If you'd rather get dressed by yourself, then wait your turn. I won't be long." He drops my hand and walks across the room and disappears into the bathroom.

My gaze follows after him. I want to go. My fingertips are actually tingling, thinking about touching him, but it's such a stupid idea. I shouldn't. Irritation shoots through me.

I storm across the room and barge in, saying, "You can't say things like that and then—" The words die in my mouth. Sean is half naked and peeling off his pants. My eyes run over his body, over the bruises and cuts that are there because of me. "You don't play fair," I choke out.

Sean grins. "Neither do you." He walks over to me and slips his hands around my waist. He tugs my hips so they line up against his naked body. "Are you going to join me or watch?"

My face flames red. *Watch?* I can't watch! What kind of person watches. Holy crap. I mill it over and realize that I'd like to watch him—no, love to watch him and his naked body in the shower. The thought jars me. I try to pull away, but he holds me tighter.

Sean grins, realizing what he did. "Ah, so you have a little bit of a voyeur thing going on?"

"No," I gasp, way too flushed. "I do not."

Sean looks down at my chest and then back at my face. "Mmm. Too bad. I think that's beyond sexy." My eyes dart anywhere and everywhere, trying to avoid his gaze. "You look a little bit guilty for someone who's telling the truth." The only thing he's wearing is a sexy smirk. I can see it out of the corner of my eye as he teases me.

My heart is pounding so fast inside my chest that it's going to explode. I glance at his shoulder, to avoid his eyes. "Guilt? This isn't guilt."

Sean tilts my chin up and our eyes meet. The floor of my stomach drops and I'm in a free fall. "Then what is it?"

I don't answer. I can't answer. I have no idea what types of sexual things I like or what I'd do. Up until now, I've done what Sean wanted. If I liked it, bonus, but I've never noticed something like this. I feel exposed and want to shy away, but Sean won't let me. We stare at each other for too long, letting the silence build. His eyes drift to my lips, but he doesn't move or release me.

I feel like I'm breathing too much. I feel like I'm drowning, but I don't want to come up for air. Sean inches closer to my lips. He hesitates there for a moment, before leaning in and taking my bottom lip between his teeth. He nips me and then drops his hands to my hips. I suck in a startled breath and allow him to move me backwards.

Sean sits me down on a little bench in front of a mirror. He looks me in the eye before he does it. Neither of us speaks. Sean's finger finds the button on my jeans. He undoes the zipper and tugs them down and pulls them off. I'm sitting in front of him in a tee shirt and panties.

Sean steps away and walks to the shower. It's directly across from me. He turns it on. Before stepping inside, he says, "Fingers between your legs, Miss Smith. Do what comes naturally. I'll leave the door open so you can see whatever entices you."

It feels like someone threw a bucket of ice water on me. I dart upright in the seat, "Sean, I can't—"

But he doesn't listen. "Yes, you can. And I think you'll like it, and I sure as hell know that I will." Then, Sean winks at me and steps into the shower.

What the hell does that mean? He really wants to watch me give myself a good time while watching his naked body in the shower? I shouldn't have thought about him and his slick skin. As soon as I do, I glance up at him and see Sean under the shower with water dripping off those toned muscles. I suck my lower lip into my mouth. I'm breathing too hard, but I can't look away. I don't want to look away.

Sean acts like I'm not there. He rubs his hands over his body, moving soap suds around before rinsing them away. After a moment, I realize that I'm no longer thinking. I'm watching. If there was a picture of a person under *voyeur* in Wikipedia, it'd be me, right now, with my jaw hanging open.

Holy hell, he's so hot. The place between my thighs is tingling uncomfortably. I think about putting my hand there, but I can't. Something holds me back.

Sean stretches and lets the water roll down his back. His arms are over his head with his hands behind his back. My eyes wander over every muscle, every perfect rise and fall of flesh. I think about feeling his skin, about running my tongue over his perfect stomach. I settle on the bench seat, leaning back against the wall, and glance at my hand. He wanted me to.

I glance back up at Sean, but he doesn't look over at me. I'm breathing so hard. It's like Sean teased the hell out of me, but he hasn't even touched me. My fingers twitch on my lap as the V at the top of my thighs demands attention. I'm caught in the middle. I want to, but I don't. My eyes remain fixed on Sean's body and more dirty thoughts race through my mind – of touching, licking, and tasting.

Any rationality I had left vacates my mind. I'm not thinking anymore. My body is all tingles and urges. I want to cross the room, walk into the shower, and throw Sean against the wall. I want to press my bare breasts into him and feel my hard nipples slide down his chest.

I stare at the curve of Sean's ass, unblinking. It's so perfect. I think about having Sean on top of me, pushing in and out, while I hold onto that perfect ass and dig my nails into his skin. It pulls vivid memories forward from the times we've been together, of the way Sean felt so hard and sharp every time he thrust into me.

When Sean turns to face the stream of water again, my gaze soaks in his perfect erection. My breath catches in my throat. I stare at him, watching him, and can't stand it anymore. My hand dips below the waistband of my panties, and over my warm skin. I press my fingers between my legs and into the slick folds of skin. My knees separate as I stroke myself, while watching Sean. His hands move over his body as the water pours off him in sheets. His eyes are closed as he tips his head back. Slowly, he moves his hand toward his long shaft and strokes. Sean's lips part as he does it again and again.

I've stopped wondering what's wrong with me, and act on my feelings. My hips thrust into my hand as I think about taking Sean's hard length in my mouth and sucking. My movements become harder and faster. I want to throw my head back, but I don't want to look away. I want to see Sean's face when he comes.

My hips slam into my hand as I rock myself higher and higher. Sean's body moves faster and faster. With every thrust into his hand, Sean's butt cheeks clench and all I can think about it biting him there. I want my tongue on his body. I want his dick in my mouth, and his hands on my breasts. My body is coiled so tight. I'm so hot. The throbbing starts and I can feel myself losing control. I think I can hold it together, but then Sean moans and thrusts hard and slow into his hand. I watch him come and see the ecstasy play out on his beautiful face.

I lose it. My head tips back and my hips buck. My fingers move faster, rubbing harder, and I shatter. Waves of ecstasy unfold inside of me. I thrust my chest higher as I hold my hand tightly between my legs. Each delicious pulse that fills my body makes me feel more sated. I stay like that for a moment, enjoying the aftershocks that are still shooting through me.

My eyelids feel heavy, but I manage to open them. When I do, Sean is standing in front of me with a wicked grin on his face. The shower is still running behind him. I didn't hear him walk over. My fingers are still inside of me with my legs spread wide open. I'm slightly horrified, but all I can do is blink.

He leans in close and whispers in my ear, "That was the sexiest thing I've ever seen. May I?"

I suck in air. All those wicked thoughts come rushing back. I don't know what he wants to do, but I nod anyway. Sean pulls my hand away and raises it to his lips. He sucks each finger before lowering his hand and dipping it into my panties. I watch him as he spreads my lower lips with his fingers and strokes me. I'm so sensitive that I gasp. I throw my head back and buck my hips at his touch. His fingers slip inside of me and I moan.

Sean sits next to me on the bench. I remain leaning back with my elbows on the make-up counter behind me. I should feel silly, sitting like this with my legs spread wide and next to this beautiful, naked, man, but I don't. I like it. I enjoy the sensations that shoot through me and refuse to think about anything else. Sean's hand teases me until I beg for release. He torments me for another moment and then gives me what I want. I cry out, saying his name, as I throb around his fingers. I feel Sean's eyes on my face, watching me as I climax. I feel his greedy gaze and know it's the same one I had when I was watching him a few moments ago.

When my breathing resumes a normal pace, I open my eyes. Sean's fingers are still inside me. He smiles and pulls his fingers out one by one, and strokes me as he pulls his hand away. The response is instant. I gasp and throw my head back. Random coils of pleasure shoot through me, pulsing softly.

My head droops back and I stare at the ceiling. Sean takes my face with one hand, holding my cheeks, and makes me look at him. His other hand appears and he moves his fingers over the seam of my lips. They're damp, from me. My lips part and he pushes a finger in, watching me intently. I suck his finger, licking it. He does it twice more before leaning in and pressing a light kiss to my mouth.

"I should have saved some for me." Sean is breathing hard. I feel his erection pressing into my leg.

I smile at him. "You make me so crazy. We weren't supposed to have sex."

"That wasn't sex." He presses his hard shaft against my leg and I smile. My girl parts clench and I think about him thrusting into me. My mind is so addled with lust, it's a fog that's growing thicker and thicker.

I manage to breathe and string some words together into a semi-coherent thought. "Since when is a hand-job not sex?"

"And you think it is because...?"

I smile awkwardly, "Because I'm supposed to charge for those." I laugh. I can't help it. Sean smiles and laughs with me.

"Mmm," he says, and kisses my neck. "That's a very reasonable answer." One of his hands is on my thigh and dips between my legs. He strokes me again and I moan. I want more. I want him.

I'm about to let him when a random part of my brain springs to life. "Wait."

Sean's hand stills and he looks me in the eye. "You wanted to start over, right? So, what does that mean? What are we?"

Sean blinks and pulls his hand away. He runs his fingers through his hair and looks over at me. "Friends, I guess."

"Damn. No wonder why you're jealous of my friends. I think you have your definitions messed up." I touch his arm lightly.

Sean looks over at me with a wry expression on his face. "Maybe."

"Try definitely. Unless you have sex with all your friends?" I'm worried for a moment. I wonder if he's slept with anyone else since he was with me. What a stupid thought. Of course he has. He ordered a hooker and got me. This guy isn't dating material...but I want him anyway.

Sean gives me a crooked smile. "Only the really hot ones." There's something about him that seems timid and uncertain. He swallows so hard that I can hear it. It's as if he's grappling with something. After a moment, Sean leans forward and rubs his hands over the back of his head. He's looking at the floor when he says, "I don't know how to do this."

"Do what?"

Sean sits up and looks at me. "You. I don't know how to be friends with you. I want you. I want to have you the way I want you, but at the same time, I can't put you through that. But I need *it*. But I want you too... I don't want to lose you." Sean seems so torn. He looks away and grips the sides of his head with his hands.

I know what he means. He's talking about his sexual needs. For a moment, I wonder if I could do it, but if he doesn't want to put me through it, I probably couldn't manage it at all. Last time he tried, I totally freaked out and I had the impression that we didn't even get started. But I want to be with him. I love him.

I slide my hand over his back. Oh my God, his skin feels so hot. I want to lean over and lick him. I banish the thoughts because they don't jive with what I'm about to say. Actually, I don't know what possesses me to say it. "Then, let's make it so you won't lose me. Be my friend. No sex, you know, like normal friends."

Sean smirks. "I don't have any normal friends. I hang out with hookers and business acquaintances."

My eyes turn into dinner plates and I stare at him. "You seriously have no friends?"

He shakes his head. "I don't have time for them. And most of them are the kind that just want something from me. Money makes it hard to have actual friends, and not just a bunch of leeches that hope I'll toss them a wad of cash."

I blink at him. "That's the saddest thing I've ever heard. What about your family?"

He shrugs. "My little brother is kind of going through something. He's never around. My parents get on me about going to a shrink whenever I see them, so I don't bother anymore. Besides that, there is no one I really care about." He looks up at me, grinning, and adds, "Except you. So, will you be my sexy friend who sometimes touches herself in front of me? Because that would make us best friends really fast." There's an absolutely wicked smile on his face.

My jaw drops open into an O. I slap his arm and laugh as my face gets hot. I can't believe he said that, even with the playful tone in his voice. I know he's joking, but it still makes me blush. "No! And never talk about this again. And get dressed. I'm not supposed to see you naked."

"But you like it." Sean grins and leans back, exposing his beautiful body.

My eyes sweep over him one last time. I know I won't be with him again. "We're not going to be naked friends. Get dressed. I'm taking a shower." I stand and walk over to the shower stall. I stop for a second when I realize that he hasn't moved. Glancing back at him, I ask, "What's the matter?"

"Nothing. You're just amazing, that's all. I've been stunned into silence and immobilized..."

I arch an eyebrow at him. "And you want to see me naked."

Sean's eyes sweep over me in a carnal way that makes my heart jump. "I already have, and it's not the kind of thing that I'll forget." He winks at me and leaves the bathroom.

My heart is hammering way too hard. I'm not sure what happened. After doing some very dirty things, I think we decided to be friends, and somehow it was my idea. I need to have my head checked.

CHAPTER 6

"Oooh! Get this one!" I throw my leg over the side of the bike after gripping the handle bars. I pull myself up onto the bike seat. The urge to say *vroom! vroom!* makes me giggle.

Sean is standing in the aisle at the motorcycle dealership. There are rows and rows of motorcycles. Some are shiny with tons of chrome, while others are bright colors and made of plastic. Sean folds his arms over his chest. "I'd need to lose my testicles first. That's a chick bike."

I straighten in the seat and cock my head. "It is not."

He laughs. "Yes, it is."

"How can you tell?"

Sean shakes his head and circles the bike before looking up at me. "One, because it's pretty, and two, because it makes you look hot. Manly men don't want pretty bikes, although I might get it for you." He reaches out and lifts the price tag dangling off the handle bars. My car is no longer running. I left it in the impound lot and don't plan on picking it up. It won't run again. I'm currently carless.

I slip off the bike. "You' not allowed to buy me anything."

"What? Are you serious?" Sean looks up at me and drops the price tag. "Why?"

I shrug and walk around the bike, dragging my fingers over the shiny paint. "I want you to be sure that I'm not hanging around for your money. I like you the way you are, demented fetishes and all." Sean's eyes darken when I mention it. The way his gaze moves over my body sends a chill up my spine. It's like his eyes are hands and I'm suddenly breathless.

I clear my throat and try to act like that didn't just happen. "So, which bike are you getting?"

Sean runs his hand through his hair and down his neck as he glances around the showroom. His eyes sweep over a ton of bikes, but he doesn't seem excited to be here. "No idea."

"Then, let's go somewhere else. Maybe the right bike isn't here. Maybe we should be on a different lot looking at minivans." The corner of my mouth tugs up as I tease him.

"Wise-ass."

"I know you like my ass, but we're talking about bikes. Jeeze, Sean. Focus." I straddle another bike and look at the shiny chrome dials. I slide my finger across the glass faces, and then take the handle bars. I say it without thinking. "Vroom! Vroom!"

Sean laughs so hard that he chokes. The salesman that Sean banished looks over at as, but doesn't say anything. Sean wipes a tear from the corner of his eye and steps toward the bike. He puts his hands around my waist and helps me down. God he smells good. "That is a dead giveaway that you're not a biker. Stop freaking out the sales guy."

Sean's hands linger a beat too long. When his fingers slip away from my waist, I turn back toward the bike. "This one is the coolest bike in here."

"You mean the prettiest."

"I mean, this is your new bike. This one." I point at it with both hands for emphasis.

"And why's that?" Sean grins, and folds his arms over his chest. He tilts his head to the side and looks the bike over. It has shiny blue paint that matches his eyes and enough chrome to make it light up like a disco ball in the sunshine.

"Because it's *so* blue, like impossibly blue. And it's huge and manly, and…" I run around to the back of the bike and pat my hand on the seat. "And look at this seat! I could totally sit here for hours. It even has a backrest!" I'm all smiles, and mouthing *buy me* when the salesman approaches.

"Did you find something you like?" Kenny is an older guy that seems too twitchy. Sean told me that he's afraid that I'll knock a row of bikes over. Kenny has gray hair and a fluffy beard like Santa Claus, but he frowns too much.

"Yes, I did." Sean's gaze is resting on me as I'm making an ass out of myself, pointing at the bike and moving my mouth in slow motion, forming silent words. It makes me stop. I purse my lips and give him a look, but Sean breaks my gaze quickly and addresses Kenny. "I'll take this one. Get it ready and set us both up with riding gear—jackets and whatever else you have."

"You are not buying me anything." I fold my arms over my chest.

Kenny looks at me and then back at Sean. Sean tilts his head toward me and adds, "I want a pair of pants, too. Leather – her size."

Kenny nods. He takes the tag off the bike and starts the paperwork.

After he leaves, I walk over to Sean. "What the hell was that?"

"What?" Sean is walking away from me, slowly walking back to the helmet displays.

I grab his arm and turn him around. "I don't want you to buy me stuff."

"And that's why I'm buying it. Besides, I want to take you for a ride and I'm not doing it if you plan on riding around in a sundress with nothing to protect you. I like this nose. I want it to stay on your face." He presses his finger to the tip of my nose when he says it and then turns and walks away. It's such a sweet gesture that it makes renders me silent.

So much for protesting, I guess I'm getting leather pants, boots, and a helmet. I'm a little excited about looking badass. I skip behind Sean and still pretend to be angry with him for ignoring my wishes, but I'm secretly saying *vroom! vroom!* in my mind and squealing like a lunatic.

CHAPTER 7

It's late by the time I get back to the dorm. I walk up the stairs to my door room and get some enthusiastic whistles from a group of guys heading down the stairs and out towards the intermural field. Apparently my butt looks mighty fine in my new leather pants. I left my helmet with Sean, but took the pants and the boots. The boots are awesome. The make me feel like Godzilla. The urge to stomp down the hallway, slamming my feet into the floor consumes me. I say screw it and stomp twice, taking two huge steps with my arms dangling in front of me like T-Rex.

"Where the hell have you been?" When I look up Mel is standing in front of me with her arms folded across her chest in the middle of the hallway. Her eyes sweep over my jacket and then down to my pants and boots. She lifts an eyebrow at me and shakes her head. "You spent the day with him, didn't you?"

The smile is still on my face. I don't care what Mel says, it's not ruining the day I had. Sean and I rode out east after he bought his bike. We ate dinner at little local place that overlooks the bay, and then he dropped me off at the dorm. It felt normal and I desperately need normal right now.

I open my mouth to reply, but Mel holds up her hand and shakes her head. "Save it, Cinderella. I don't want to hear the stupid shit going through your mind."

"Mel," I groan. I try to push past her to go to my room, but she catches the crook of my arm.

"Damn it, Avery. I'm serious. You nearly got crushed by a semi the other night. You gotta be more careful, and hanging out with that demented biker is not anybody's idea of careful. I already screamed at Fairy-boy for letting you go. Sean is off limits. Got it?" Mel's in my face and her manicured finger is poking me in the chest.

My eyebrows disappear under my bangs as I swat her hand away. "Throwing himself under a truck didn't redeem him, did it?"

"No," she snaps. "And one good act doesn't undo all the other stupid shit he's done. The man is bad news. He's messing with your mind and you're letting him."

I sigh, and push past her. Mel follows me down the hallway. "Avery, I'm just watching out for you. So much stuff has been going on. Damn it, listen to me!" Mel grabs my shoulders and spins me around. "I'm the only one who knows what you've gone through and what you're doing. Don't waste it like this. If Black finds out that you've been seeing him, you'll lose everything."

My smile is gone. I don't say anything for a second. I know she's right, I just wish she wasn't. I need that job to dig myself out of the ever-increasing hole I keep digging. As it is, I'm sure I'm on her shit list. I close my eyes and say it, "Fine. You're right."

"Don't try pulling that reverse mind shit on me, I know I'm right!"

"Mel, back off. I said I agree with you. I can't lose my job."

Mel finally deflates. She nods slowly and grabs my wrist. She drags me down the hallway and into her room. After slamming the door, she rounds on me. "Black has you on the schedule for next weekend. I saw it when I went in today to get my contract for the week."

It feels like all the air was sucked out of the room. I didn't expect her to put me back so fast, even though I asked. I haven't even spoken to Black since before the accident. Although I sent Gabe back with a wad of cash and demanded to be reinstated, I didn't expect her to actually do it.

"Who'd she put me with?"

"I don't know." Mel sits down hard on her bed and looks up at me. She pushes her huge hair out of her face and sighs. "What are you planning on doing?"

"With what?" I sit down in her chair and pull my boots off. Mel notices them but doesn't say anything.

"With Black. I know it was supposed to be a stopgap job until graduation, but then you need to do your graduate work. I know I have to keep that job until I'm done and making it on my own. I'm guessing that you need to do the same thing, so you need to stay on Black's good side. You had a bumpy start, Avery. I'm shocked she hasn't fired your ass."

I haven't really thought past graduation, about what I'll do. I keep getting stuck in now. I glance up at Mel. "So what do I do?"

"Kiss her ass. Take whatever clients she gives you and make them rave about you."

I smile awkwardly. "I don't have the skills to—"

"Then learn! Take the initiative. Rent some porn. Go to that sex shop everyone's always talking about. Look around. Watch a pole dance. Do something that makes you so desirable that the clients beg for you and only you."

"What do you do?"

She laughs under her breath. "Stuff that you can't pull off, white girl. I'm me, in all my mocha sexual hotness. I own it. I own him. I have him eating out of my hand before I leave. I make sure to put it in his head that there's more. It's all bullshit, but when they're like that, none of the guys are really thinking with their head. They let their pants make all the decisions. String them along. Fake it 'til you make it and all that shit." Mel lies back on her bed and stuffs a pillow under her head. She sighs like she's exhausted.

"I'm sorry," I blurt out. I know the reason why she's overtired and strung out. It's me.

Mel waves her hand in the air. "Nah, no sorry's. There are no do-overs for girls like us. We're one shot wonders. I know that. I've been through shit you can't even imagine and I have no intention of giving up. I know what's at the very bottom when you fall flat on your face. I just don't want you going through that, not when you don't have to. And I know this guy makes you happy sometimes, but he's driving me nuts.

He's risking stuff you don't have to risk. You get what I'm saying to you?"

I nod. "I get it." My voice is totally flat.

All the happy vibes from earlier are gone. I feel guilt tugging at me every time my eyes glance at my boots or my hand touches my leather pants. She's right. Mel's so right and I've gotten so careless. I push off the chair and tell her, "Thanks. I'm glad you're on my side. I need to go study for a test in the morning. I'll catch you at lunch tomorrow."

I walk away wondering what horrors Mel's been through that I don't know about. Whenever she's warning me, I see the memories replay on her face. There's fear in her eyes and nothing can take it away. I don't want to get like that, and the best way to prevent it is to do what Mel said—suck up to Black, kiss Sean good-bye, and start taking new clients.

I just don't want to...

CHAPTER 8

The rest of the week passes slowly. I go to classes and try to focus, but it takes an ungodly amount of coffee. I don't see Sean. I try not to think about him. I do my work and keep my nose in my books until I get a call from Miss Black. She has a client for me. I have to go in and chat with her before she forks over his name. Black sounds more irritated with me than normal. I tell her that I'll be in tonight and hang up before I say something stupid.

I've been sitting in the diner across the street from the college, working on the outline for my semester project in Psych. I have a textbook open with colored highlighters on the table, and Post-It Notes stuck all over the book. They stick out of the sides like rainbow colored bunny ears. I'm not paying attention to who's around me. When the waitress comes by, I order more coffee and a slice of apple pie.

"Do you want ice cream with that, hun?" She stares down at me from under a boat-load of blue eye shadow.

Marty appears from behind her and answers for me. "Hell yes. And double that. I'm sick of watching my figure. Today has pie and ice cream written all over it, honey." The waitress looks at him like he's smacked his head one to many times. Marty makes a face at her and she leaves. "Long time, no see. Whachya doing, slut?" Marty leans forward and tries to see my notes from across the table.

I smile at him. "Term paper. What's new with you?" I look him over. He's not dressed in his normal decade-specific attire. Instead, Marty's hair is sort of messy and he has a little stubble on his jaw. He's wearing a button down shirt with a dark brown blazer. It makes his eyes look like chocolates. "Got a new boyfriend?"

He smiles awkwardly and shakes his head. "Nah."

"What's with the new threads? Trying to channel GQ?"

Marty tilts his chin up and grins. "Something like that. You like?"

I nod and let my eyes slip over him again, before returning my gaze to his face. "Yeah, actually I do. It's hot. Sure to turn a lot of heads." I smile at him and glance back down at my outline. I'm almost done and I've been working for hours, so I push the book aside and take a break.

"Mmm. Maybe, but there's only one head that I'm interested in turning." He stretches and places one of his arms along the back of the booth.

"Does he notice you?" Marty doesn't talk much about his love interests. I'd started thinking he was asexual. I'm glad we're talking. It feels like it used to, before things got weird between us.

"Not so much." He holds my gaze.

"That's too bad."

"Maybe. Maybe not. Everything happens for a reason, right? Maybe it's not time to be noticed, yet. Maybe when I am noticed, things will go better because I waited. At least that's what I tell myself when I'm crying into my pillow at night." He winks at me. Before I have a chance to answer, the waitress sets down our plates. Marty sits up and inhales. He sighs, "My God. Ecstasy on a plate."

The waitress snorts and walks away.

I dig in and shovel the pie into my mouth. The apples are warm and the crust is light and buttery. I think I moaned because Marty's laughing. "Easy there, Little Miss O. I'm not into that kind of public display."

I nearly choke on an apple. I sputter for a second. "You're such an ass. You can make sexual remarks about dessert, but I can't?"

"Yes." Marty shovels more pie into his mouth, while watching me with a smirk on his face.

"Why is that?"

"Double-standard, honey. I can do a lot of things you can't. I don't have boobs. Get over it." He glances around and holds up his hand. The waitress comes over. "Can I get a glass of milk? Thanks, hon." She smiles this time and disappears. A few minutes later there's a huge glass of milk next to him. I salivate, staring at it. "Go ahead and have some. I don't have cooties." Marty shoves the glass toward me. I put the cold cup to my lips and guzzle. When I put it down, there's hardly any left. "Well, that was sexy."

"Shut up," I say, smiling at him. "I can be sexy. I just chose not to be."

"Who said that wasn't sexy? A girl tipping back a glass of milk like that? Very alluring." He waggles his eyebrows at me. "Any girl that can swallow that much milk has gotta be good at—"

I cut him off, pointing my spoon at him. "Don't say it." There's a warning tone in my voice.

But Marty is still smiling. He shakes his head. "You're such a prude. You can put out and get paid, you little tramp, but we can't talk about it. I thought I'd hear all about your sexual encounters. I'm starting to think your job is bogus." Marty leans back in the booth with a self-assured look on his face.

"It is not *bogus*. And who uses that word anymore?"

"Nuns and cool kids. Stop dodging the question, princess." He leans forward and puts his arms on the table. Marty reaches forward and places both of his hands on top of mine and pats me.

"Uh, there was no question."

He cocks his head to the side. "Avery, are you seriously going to make me say it. Fine, the blank look on your face is enough. Are you going back to work this weekend?" He slips his hands back.

I nod. "Yeah, Black wants me to come in tonight. I think she's going to kill me and leave me in the alley. She sounds pissed. I'm not really sure why."

"You're a high-maintenance pain in the ass, that's why. Every time she gives you another chance, you screw it up. It's like you're doing it on purpose."

"I am not! I want this job. I need this job."

He studies me for a moment. "You really don't mind the idea of it being some random guy this time?" I mind. I mind a lot, but it's the best I can do. It's like he can read my mind. Marty leans forward and lowers his voice, "Then, don't do it. Quit."

"What? Did you hit your head? I can't quit. I'm going to get hit with a ton of hospital bills, plus my regular stuff. My car is totaled. I don't have enough money to replace it and eat. It's not like I have a choice, Marty."

He sighs and watches me for a moment. "Then, tell me how I can help."

"I don't think you can, not unless you want to go shopping again. I have to but a slutty outfit tomorrow. No more wholesome girl stuff. Mel isn't around tonight. She took a midweek client. You want to come?" Marty's eyes drop to the table. He looks at my hands and seems like he's lost in his thoughts. "It'll be the same as last time, well, without Mel calling you names."

I realize that I want him to come. Marty is one of the people that puts me at ease, and this stuff with Black has me strung out. I don't want a new client. I want Sean, but I can't have what I want. Besides, Sean probably had a different girl every day this week. They're probably all tied up under his bed.

Marty touches the back of my hand. He trails his finger over my smooth skin. The touch pulls me from my thoughts. I look up at his face, into those dark eyes. "I'll come. Anything for you, Avery. You know that."

I let out a rush of air. I didn't realize I was so tense about everything. I slip out of the booth and go around to his side. I slide in next to him and give him a hug. He doesn't hug me back. Instead he puts his arm behind my neck and rests it along the back of the booth.

Marty pushes the rest of his pie toward me. "Here, finish it."

I release him and sit up. I devour the rest of the pie like I haven't eaten in weeks. My life is finally getting under control again.

CHAPTER 9

"What about this one?" Marty asks, pulling out a tiny hanger with a red string on it. Seriously, it's a string. I don't even know what it is. A bottom? A bra? A shirt?

I walk over and touch it, then look up at him. Leaning in close, I ask, "What is it?"

He laughs. "I don't know. I was hoping you knew."

We both giggle quietly and put it back. I'm in one of the shops that Miss Black said to buy my lingerie in, but I don't know what I want. It's weird. Last time I did this, I thought of Sean and bought things that I wanted him to see me in. This time, I don't even know who I'm going to be with. I guess I should pick out things for me, but I'm not really into it.

Marty wanders away, browsing racks. He picks up something white and I shake my head. I'm not making that mistake again. I tell him about the rules and he nods and wanders off. When I turn around, I see a red satin bra that seems cut so low that it wouldn't contain my girls. I lift the hanger and hold it up.

A salesgirl comes over. "Do you like it? That's one of our bestsellers." I turn around. The salesgirl is a little taller than me, wearing a stunning blue dress that makes her hair look like gold. She's smiling at me. "Would you like to try it on?"

I nod, "I think so. It seems a little low in front."

"It's supposed to be." She smiles at me and must recognize the blank look on my face, because she explains. "It's a hybrid shelf and peek-a-boo bra. It holds you up, creates beautiful cleavage, but is still revealing. The panty you had before is the matching bottom."

"The string?"

She nods and picks up the red string. "It wraps around the side, after you step into it. Then, tie it on the hip." She selects pieces that are my size. "Is there anything else you'd like to try?"

I glance around. "I don't know." *Where'd Marty go?*

"Is there something in particular that you're looking for?" I tell her something sexy and she makes a few more selections for me.

On the way back to the dressing room, I see Marty. He falls in step with me. "Try this one too." He hands me something blue. I nod and take it.

The salesgirl doesn't say anything about Marty following me back. I think about that red set and worry about him seeing me in it. I don't really care about him seeing me in my underwear, but exposed nipples with those bottoms—I don't know. Gay or not, that's a little bit overexposed for my preference.

The salesgirl hangs my items in a room and leaves. Marty finds a chair and sits down across from my changing room. "Okay, show me the blue one first."

That's the set he picked out. It's also the one with the most coverage. No problem, although I know Black will shoot down the bottoms. I have to show off my ass from now on. I'm not a virgin anymore.

I slip out of my clothes and pull on a blue satin set. It is pretty, but it's too plain for this. I crack the door and call Marty over. He slips into the dressing room with me. "Turn around, let me see." Marty nods as he rubs his chin. "It's too old school for this, but it is pretty."

I look at my hips in the mirror. Old school is right. The boobs are kind of pointy. I laugh. "I look like Marilyn Monroe."

"If they were just a bit pointier, I would have said Madonna."

"Okay, this one is out."

Marty cracks the door to step outside. I glance over his shoulder and see a familiar face standing in the store just outside the dressing room. Bright blue eyes catch my gaze. My heart hammers harder.

Sean.

He holds my gaze for a moment and then blinks like he didn't just see Marty come out of my dressing room. Marty doesn't notice him, and I don't want him to. I try to get rid of Marty quickly. The last thing I want is the two of them fighting back here, and since they both seem to hate each other, it's pretty much a sure thing.

"Marty, would you mind heading to the second floor to scout out a dress? I'm pretty sure I'm going to want the red panty set and I'm not showing you my ass."

He chuckles. "Sure, babe. What color?"

"Red." I blurt it out and shut the door. Marty's feet disappear from sight. I lean against the door. My shoulders tense as I listen for the altercation, but it doesn't come.

I sigh and push off the door. I don't know where Sean went, but at least he had the decency to not make a scene. It probably looked like Marty was doing me in the dressing room. My cheeks burn. I wouldn't want anyone to think that. Then, I realize that everyone probably thinks that. I'm so slow. I palm my face and shake my head.

Damn it. I'm so stupid. I guess it doesn't matter, but I don't want word getting back to Black that I was doing some guy in the dressing room. I need to keep my personal life separate. I wonder if that's possible as I slip out of the panty set and try on another.

I turn and glance at my hips and then my butt. My boobs look okay, but I don't like it. I try on the last two normal sets of lingerie. I stare at myself in the mirror wondering if it matters what I wear. Who cares if I like it or not?

I glance at the red set still hanging on the wall.

I slip out of my clothes and reach for it. I step into the string bottoms and tie a bow at my hip.

Seriously? A string doesn't change the fact that this is commando. The guy is going to get an eyeful as soon as I'm out of my dress. As I'm taking the top off the hanger, the door creaks opens slowly.

"I'm in here." I can't decide if I should cover myself or stop the door. My hands wave around like I'm dancing and Sean slips into the room.

"I know." The grin on his face is so wide. I twitch and cover my breasts with my arm. When I catch myself in the mirror, I groan.

He smirks. "You look like you could use some help."

"I don't need your help. Go away." I want to push him out the door, but then I'd have to flash my boobs at him and I don't want to. "Scat."

"Scat? Seriously? You're going to throw me out, but you let him in?" Sean's tone is light, playful. He glances around the room and walks over to the things that I've already tried on. They are in a pile on the padded bench against the wall.

"He's gay—"

"Keep telling yourself that—"

"Oh my god. You are unbelievable. You're jealous of a gay guy." I tilt my head to the side and give him my best are-you-fucking-serious face, but I'm naked—so he laughs.

"Damn, you're cute." Sean takes the red bra from where I dropped it on the floor and looks at it. "I'm not jealous. I just don't like liars and I don't want anyone to hurt you. Turn around."

"Sean—" I try to protest but he turns me toward the mirror. I don't drop my arm.

"I've already seen and had them, Avery. Drop your arm." Sean is standing behind me with the bra in his hands. I'm stubborn. I feel my spine straightening. I don't want to do it. I don't want him here, but part of me does. Part of me likes this. Part of me is obviously defective.

"Fine," I bite back, "but this didn't happen. My friends hate your guts and I don't want Black to know I've been talking to you."

Sean gives me a lopsided grin as he reaches around me and slips the bra on. His fingers brush against my skin as he fastens it in back. Involuntarily, I suck in a sharp breath at the light touch. I'm staring at myself in the mirror, with Sean—who is fully dressed and beyond beautiful— standing behind me. My stomach curls and I feel hot. I glance away, hoping he doesn't notice, but now I'm noticing everything. I'm breathing too much, too loudly. I don't know where to put my hands, but they feel stupid dangling at my sides. But the worst part is this bra. The front holds me up and adds a cup size, which makes my taut nipples glaringly obvious.

Sean looks up into the mirror, but he doesn't step back. I feel his breath on my skin and resist the urge to climb on him. Because that's what I want to do. With him here, looking at me like that, and standing so close—oh God—I want to touch him and feel his skin under my fingertips. I wish he wasn't so fucked up. Or maybe, I wish I was more messed up so I could let him do what he wanted, but I can't. I shiver thinking about it.

I see Sean's gaze in the mirror. It locks with mine. After a moment, he says, "Is this for a client?"

"Yes." There's a lump in my throat that won't go away. My fingers twitch at my sides. I want to touch him. I wish he'd turn me around, but he doesn't. Sean stands so close that we should be touching, but we aren't. Every inch of my skin is sensitive, dying for contact.

"It needs something else." Sean pulls a bag out of his pocket. He must have purchased something before he came back. "This is what I'd want to see you in." I take the bag. Sean's fingers brush against mine. My heart pounds harder. I suck in air like I haven't taken a breath in five minutes. It's too loud, too raspy. "Open it."

I look into the bag. There's a black box at the bottom. I take it out and open it. Inside are two silver rings shaped in a C. There's a single crystal on each one. I look up at him.

He smiles at me. "Put them on."

My stomach flips. His voice is so much deeper. It's that voice that makes me do stupid things. I take one out of the box and look at it. I'm not sure what it is, but it looks like an earring, so I pull my hair back and go to put it on my ear.

Sean smiles and takes my hand. He steps closer to me, pressing his front against my back. Sean moves my hand to my breast and breathes, "It goes here."

His hand is on top of mine. I'm staring at him in the mirror, frozen. My brain is ringing warning bells, but I can't move. After a moment, he turns me toward him and takes the jewelry from me. "Allow me."

Sean leans closer to me and slides his hand up my waist. He cups the bottom of my breast and slips his hand over my nipple. My back goes ram-rod straight. My voice disappears as a bolt of heat shoots between the V of my legs. Sean rolls my nipple between his fingers, teasing it, before putting the silver C on me. Then, he squeezes it gently and the silver pinches me. I gasp silently as my lips make a little O. Sean watches my expression as he does the same thing to my other nipple. Then, he takes my shoulders and turns me back to the mirror.

"There you go, bestie. A totally fuckable outfit for a fun Friday night."

My chest swells as it fills with air. It forces my breasts out and the little crystals sparkle. I look in the mirror and love this outfit because he likes it. I can't speak. I can't think. I stare at my breasts too long. When my eyes lift to see Sean's in the mirror, I notice the same dark look he had the other morning.

Sean steps closer to me. His lips are so close to my neck. I tip my head to the side, hoping he'll kiss me. I want him to touch me, but he doesn't. I refuse to move. I don't need him. I can control myself. But, Sean doesn't leave. He doesn't talk and his eyes remain hooded, as he drinks in my reflection. Every inch of my body is buzzing. I'm wound so tight that I think I'll snap. That's when Sean's hand slowly drifts up my thigh without touching. I sense the heat from his palm. It makes my skin tingle and ache for his touch. Sean stops just above the bow on my hip. His fingers flick the string. I close my eyes and suck in a shaky breath.

"Ask me," he breathes. Defiance strums through me. Or maybe it's pride. Or both. Whatever it is, I say nothing which makes Sean give me the most seductive grin I've ever seen. "I know you want it. Ask me, Avery... "

I suck my lower lip between my teeth and slowly shake my head, *no*.

Sean doesn't back away. Instead, he takes hold of the string at my hip and pulls. The red bow comes undone and my indecent bottoms fall to the dressing room floor. Sean watches me in the mirror. His eyes dip to the floor and linger as they climb up my body. They stop at the top of my legs and he leans in close and whispers again, "Ask me."

I shake my head, liking this game. My heart pounds harder, as Sean looks up at my face. I wonder what he's going to do. His eyes are so dark, so impossibly blue. Sean moves his hands over my skin without touching me. Slowly he goes up my thigh and then down my belly. His shirt tickles my back as he reaches around me. His warm breath makes me want to melt into his kiss, but I don't move. I remain silent.

Sean continues to tease me. As his hands move over my body, his lips hoover over my back. His hot breath trails a path down my back, caressing every curve until he's on his knees. Sean touches my leg lightly and sparks shoot across my body.

I gasp, and turn so that he's kneeling in front of me. He looks up at me with his eyes burning like blue flames. "Ask me."

I smile and shake my head so slightly that I'm not sure if I moved. Sean blinks slowly and lowers his gaze. He leans in slow, his lips nearing my thigh, and hesitates. I feel like I'm going to explode. I've never wanted to be touched so much in my entire life. Sean's warm breath hits my bare skin and sparks shoot through me, making me hotter and hotter. My core aches for his touch, for Sean, and he hasn't even touched me yet. I'm a hot mess, ready to beg him to kiss me there, but I don't have to. After a heart pounding moment, Sean takes a jagged breath.

This time when he looks up, he says something different. "I'm asking you—may I?" His eyes fall back to the prize right in front of his eyes.

I have no voice. I can't breathe. I feel myself nod and then my world shifts. Sean's hands are on me and I moan so loudly that he reaches up and puts his hand over my mouth. He looks me in the eye and shakes his head slowly, telling me to be silent.

When Sean releases his hand, he lowers me onto the bench and falls to his knees.

Sean crawls toward me and nuzzles his face between my legs. I suck in air and throw my head back, careful not to make and sounds. Sean breathes me in before taking his hands and pushing my knees farther apart. He looks at me with those sinful eyes and then disappears between my legs.

His tongue strokes my hot folds with big greedy licks. I bite my lip to keep quiet and squirm in my seat. Sean's hands come up and hold me still as he pushes his tongue in deeper. Somehow my legs end up over his shoulders and I'm holding his hair between my fingers, pulling his face toward me. I fight to remain silent. My hips rock slightly as Sean's tongue devours me.

I make little sounds that drive him crazy and he pushes into me deeper. Butterflies float through my middle and tickle my stomach. Hot tendrils curl tighter and move through me. I can't let go of him. Sean comes up for air and it makes me beg for more. He gives me a wicked grin before lavishing my lower lips with more wet kisses.

I rock against his mouth as he devours me. Neither of us makes a sound. I feel my body responding to his touches, climbing higher and higher. Every time Sean's tongue thrusts inside me, I feel my body getting closer to the edge. Sean teased me so much that it'll take next to nothing to tip me over the top. His tongue sweeps against me again and again.

I hold Sean against me, pushing my hips toward his mouth, wanting him to push me over the edge. But Sean slows his pace and pulls back. I whimper, as his kisses soften. He takes my hands from the side of his head and pins them by my hips on the bench and stops.

I buck my hips, desperately wanting the release, and beg him, "Please. Oh please."

Sean smiles at me. He watches my face for a moment, and watches me breathe. My breasts strain against the bra and the nipple clips feel so tight. It makes me want him even more. Without warning, Sean dips between my legs again. He releases my hands and grips the curve of my ass, forcing my soft skin to his lips. I hold onto him and rock. Sean's tongue dips into me over and over again, and I shatter. Every tightly wound coil inside of me breaks free as my body pulses uncontrollably. I breathe harder and harder, as he continues to draw out my pleasure. Sean's tongue sweeps against me, dipping inside as I float away in bliss.

My hold on Sean loosens as his licking slows. When Sean pulls away, he stands and leans in, and sweeps his moist lips across my mouth. "That's the second time this week I've watched you come and I didn't get to fuck you either time."

I laugh. There's a lazy sated smile on my face. "You're horrible."

"You're delicious." He licks his lips slowly.

"Avery? Are you still in there?" Marty's voice rings out and suddenly I'm fully alert. I press my finger to my lips and hope Sean doesn't say anything.

I clear my throat and try to sound normal. "Yeah. I'll be up in a second."

"Okay, just checking. It's been a while." His voice is so close. I know he's right on the other side of the door. I don't want to explain Sean, and I know Marty will kill me if he knows what I just did.

Sean is quietly watching me as I lie to one of my best friends. My eyes pinch shut. "Sorry. I found something else I wanted to try. I'll be right up."

"Yeah," Marty says, but his voice doesn't sound right. I think he knows, but Marty walks away without another word.

I sigh and sit down hard on the little bench and bury my face in my hands. Sean is standing, looking down at me. "I don't like lying to him."

"Then don't."

I laugh, but there's no humor in it. "I can't. Marty and Mel don't want me around you. They think you're going to…" my voice trails off and I look up at him.

Sean finishes the sentence for me. "Hurt you."

I nod. "It's more than that, though. Mel doesn't even want me to be your friend. Maybe that's because she knows that I can't. Damn it, Sean. Things can't be like this." I stand and pull on my panties. I take the clips off and put them back in the black case. I finish getting dressed.

While I'm dressing, he says nothing. Sean just leans against the back wall of the dressing room with his hands behind his back. When I look over at him, there's a pensive expression on his face. I throw my purse on my shoulder before grabbing the black box and holding it out to Sean.

He doesn't move. He doesn't pull his hands out from behind his back and take them. Instead he shakes his head. "No, you need those. They complete your outfit for work. Wear them."

My stomach dips. How can he act so detached? Sean's talking about another guy having sex with me, and it's like he doesn't care. "What are you doing?"

Sean straightens. His eyes narrow as he looks at me. I have no idea what he's thinking. "I don't know what you mean."

"Yes, you do. Don't give me that crap. How can you possibly be okay with sharing me?"

"I'm not okay with sharing you. I don't like it at all, but I can't ask you to stop. It's something you need. I understand that. The guy that's always drooling on your shoulder, I can't stand." He's so frustratingly calm that I want to punch him in the face. Sean blinks at me like I'm crazy.

"You don't want me hanging out with Marty, but I can go fuck a client?" Sean nods slowly. His dark hair falls forward with the movement. Sean looks at his shoe before returning his gaze to my face.

"You're lying." I step toward him and get up in his face. Sean's lips are a breath away. His eyes are intently focused, our gazes lock. "You don't want to share me at all. You're trying to get me fired."

"I could have kept you. I didn't."

"Things got too serious and you chickened out."

"Your perception of reality is skewed, Miss Smith. You better blink and wake up from that dream of yours."

I laugh once, hard. He's pushing every button I have and I don't know why. Sean does this every time I mention anything about labeling what we are. I reel in my anger and cut my gaze to the floor. When I look back up at him, I breathe, "You're the one who needs to stop dreaming, Mr.

Jones. One day I won't be there when you need me, I won't magically show up, and I won't give you another chance."

Sean doesn't blink. I'm lost in his eyes for a moment. There's something there, a wall that I can't get past. I wonder if he'll ever let me in, if he'll ever tell me what happened to him that made him this way. Sean finally looks away. He lowers his head and steps back. His silence irritates me. Sean doesn't offer any explanation or anything.

I make an annoyed sound and reach for the door. Just as my hand lands on the knob, Sean takes my wrist. I look back at him. Sean doesn't lift his gaze. Instead he stares at my hand, in his grip. "There's no future for us, but I don't want to let you go."

"Then, change your future. Let someone in. You're doing this to yourself and I was stupid enough to go along with it." Sean looks up at me and I'm screwed. All my resolve melts and washes away because there's genuine fear in his eyes. He's afraid he's going to lose me. "Sean…"

He nods slowly. "I'm trying, I swear to God, I am. I haven't—I'm trying to let you in, Avery. Don't give up, not yet. Come by my place after work."

I smile sadly and shake my head. "That's a really bad idea."

"You said to change, so I'm changing. I'm trying. I want to hang out with my friend after work. We'll have ice cream and watch movies. You can bitch about your boss or do whatever you want. I won't even try to seduce you."

I smirk. "Sean—"

He rubs his thumb over the back of my hand and says, "Please, Avery. Give me more time."

I'm a sucker. His words crumble what's left of my will. "All right. I'll see you later."

He nods and kisses the back of my hand. Before I step outside, I turn back and ask, "Are you, uh, still tormenting hookers for fun?"

Sean gives me a strange look, then he steps toward me. "If you mean, will I be having company before you come over, the answer is yes. I won't do those things with you, but I still need it."

I lower my gaze. It feels weird. I knew he didn't stop. I just wished he had. I wished that I was enough to pull Sean back from that, but I guess I'm not. There's too much darkness in him.

Sean rubs the back of my hand lightly. "It's better this way, right? We both get what we need, and share the best part of us with each other."

I nod in agreement, but I don't agree. The thing that pulled me to Sean was the darkness, the enormous stain on his soul, and the reason was simple—it matches mine. Sometimes I feel like we're linked, like our pain is so intense when we're alone, but when we come together it cancels out. Maybe I'm dreaming. Maybe it's not really like that. Maybe we're both destined to be alone.

CHAPTER 10

I blink and look up at Miss Black like she has two heads. "You want me to see Henry again?"

Miss Black is standing by the glass table in the corner. I'm seated and staring at Henry's file. He was really sweet, but I don't understand why I haven't been reinstated. Henry wasn't into sex, he just wanted a date for a business meeting.

Miss Black touches her temple gingerly, like I'm giving her headache. Gabe walks by slowly and shakes his head once, very carefully, so Miss Black doesn't see. I'm not sure what he means, so I take it as a sign to shut up, tell Miss Black thank you, and get the hell out of there.

"Avery, quite honestly, I don't know what to do with you. Your first client is stalking you and your second client appears to be equally infatuated with you."

"Mr. Ferro isn't stalking me."

Miss Black turns and raises a perfectly plucked brow. I shut my mouth, and she continues. "I don't know what is going on with you. Either, you're very good at your job or you're a train wreck. There's no middle ground with you.

"Gabe watched you manage the disastrous date and said you handled it extremely well. All parties left the restaurant without killing each other. Actually, Gabe said both men left *happy*. How you did that is mindboggling, because whenever we speak, it seems like you have no idea what you're doing. It's almost as if you're completely inept right up until the moment that you're thrown into the situation.

Frankly, it makes me nervous, which is why I'm handing you back to Mr. Thomas.

"This isn't for arm candy this time, Miss Stanz. It's the full package. I want to remind you that your preference sheet has no limits. Do you want to update it?"

My heart is pounding. Gabe's warning is playing through my mind. I can't lose this job. I shake my head. "No, I'll leave it."

Miss Black smiles smoothly, like she's pleased. "There are only two women who work with me that have their preferences wide open, and you're one of them. I'm pleased with your decision. Remember to wear your bracelet. Have you been taking your birth control pills?" I nod. I'm not an idiot. "Good. I don't want you knocked up just when you get the hang of things.

"Gabe will be discretely overseeing the first part of your evening, tomorrow. Check in afterward. If you do well, I'll give you another client this weekend. Do you have any questions?"

I shake my head and keep my eyes down. My fingers twitch by my sides. I'm nervous. This whole thing makes me anxious. It's real now, so much more so than when I accepted Sean as a client. I've agreed to be with two different men this weekend, and to do anything they want. I must have lost my mind.

Miss Black hands me a card. "This is the fee for tomorrow evening. Assuming you complete this contract, you'll be paid the next morning. The rate is higher because of your preference sheet, and because your services become increasingly expensive if the same client keeps asking for you." Miss Black snaps her fingers and turns. She strides toward her office, saying, "Follow me."

When she shuts the door, I stand in the middle of the room. Miss Black sits behind her desk. She looks stressed. "Come on. We don't have all night. Show me what you're going to wear tomorrow."

"The dress is for the date and…" I slip off the tight red cocktail dress and show her the lingerie. My heart is pounding. This feels so strange. I thought it would get easier as I came in here more often and talked to her, but it's getting more uncomfortable. Maybe it's because my outfits are becoming more *hookerish* and less *Averyish*.

Miss Black's eyes sweep over me as I turn once. When I look back at her, she laughs and shakes her head. "You do some things perfectly. This is perfection. I like the crystals. If you had more, you'd look like a showgirl, but just the way they are is classy. Well done." After opening a desk drawer, Black shoos me. I don my dress and bolt.

When I get to the elevator, I press the button and wait. When the doors open, Gabe is inside. He doesn't say anything as we ride down, but he walks me outside.

When we walk through the door, he says, "You're on thin ice with her. Be careful." He nods at me once and walks away.

I know I have to make Henry the happiest man alive tomorrow night. I just don't know how to do it.

CHAPTER 11

After my classes are done on Friday, I meet up with Mel and Marty at the diner. Having money is nice. I can afford to eat.

We're well into our meal when Marty says, "So, who's hooking tonight?" He puts down his huge glass of milk and grins at us. Mel is sitting next to me in the booth. She kicks him under the table. "Owh!"

"You have no class," Mel says and takes another bite of her BLT.

Marty straightens and clears his throat. He presses his hand to his puffed up chest and says in a bad British accent, "I'm sorry, dear lady. Will you be entertaining gentlemen callers this evening? I'm asking because my weekends have gotten dreadfully dull since you both endeavored into the business of ill repute." He breaks character and adds, "Well, except for last weekend when we thought Avery was a road pancake."

"No class at all." Mel puts down her food and shakes her head. "No wonder you can't find a boyfriend. You're too dense to notice when you're offending the more delicate sex."

Marty laughs once, loudly. Putting his hands on the table, he leans forward, "Nothing about you is delicate, Mel. You're all thorns and nails. Piss and vinegar is too mild to describe you."

I'm lost in my own little world while they go back and forth. I don't like the idea of seeing Sean after he's been with someone. I don't like the idea of being with someone while he's with someone else. We should be with each other. I wonder about

Sean, about what he'd do to me and how far he'd push me to get what he wants. The thought scares me. Sean honed in on my claustrophobia quickly. If he tied me up and threw me in a closet, I think I'd cry. It's not sexy. I can't connect the two. They don't fit together.

Marty stops grinning and looks at me. "Are you nervous, kitten?"

I blink and look up. I didn't realize he was talking to me. Marty and Mel have been arguing since we sat down. I haven't said much of anything. "No, I'm just not looking forward to it."

"Is it someone new?" Mel asks.

I shake my head. "No, same guy as last week."

"Well, that should be good, right?" Marty looks at Mel and then back at me. "Someone fill me in if it's not good."

"It's awkward, that's all," I say, and poke my salad.

Mel glances over at me. "Wanna do something after work? I need some chillaxing time with my girls." Mel tilts her chin up toward Marty and adds, "That includes you too, fruit cup."

He gives Mel a girly grin then lifts his glass. "I wanna bring my new nightie!"

Mel rolls her eyes and looks over at me. I haven't said anything. "So, you up for it?"

They're both looking at me. I need to lie really good and I suck at it. My brain flashes my blank preference sheet at me. The words are rolling off my tongue before I can blink. "I'll have to take a rain check. I've got an all-nighter, so I doubt I'll be back until morning."

Mel smiles at me and nods. "Good for you. That'll be good money, Avery. You're back on track. No distractions."

Marty grins. "I think she had a bit of a *distraction* when we were shopping the other day." I blink at him. If he knows and tells Mel, I'll kill him.

Mel's gaze is burning a hole in the side of my face. "I told you to stay away from him! Avery, damn it. Do you need a helmet? Are you that mentally impaired? Fuck girl, I—"

Marty flinches when he sees Mel's reaction, and cuts her off. "Back off, psycho. I was just kidding. The saleslady thought me and Avery did it in the dressing room. As if." He makes a super gay gesture and winks at me, like it's the most preposterous thing he's ever heard.

Mel's still tense. She snaps at Marty some more. I can't stand the two of them fighting, not when I feel so strung out. I slip out of the booth and throw some money on the table. "I need to go get ready and if I don't beat Amber back, she'll lock me out of the room. I'll catch up with you on Sunday. We'll do IHOP."

Mel grins and rubs her hands together. "Pancakes!"

"You are such a pancake whore." Marty giggles at Mel and she winks at him. They both start laughing as I walk away from the table.

———

I dress quickly before Amber gets back from dinner. The little red dress makes me feel exposed. I run down the back staircase and push out the back door before I look around for Gabe. He's picking me up until I figure out what to do about transportation. I don't have any credit and I don't have enough money to buy anything. Black told Gabe to pick me up in the meantime.

When I push out the back door, I walk into the parking lot and stop in my tracks. I blink once, hard.

My car.

I blink again, rapidly, and walk towards it. I haven't seen it since the accident. It wasn't running and the front was smashed up. But, I'm looking at it now and the car looks the way it did before the accident. I glance and see Gabe pull into the parking lot. I walk towards my car quickly, holding up a finger for him to wait. I peer inside and see an envelope on the seat. I open the door and grab it.

Standing outside my car, I rip it open and read.

> *It's not new, so it doesn't count as a present.* -S

I smile and shove the note into my purse, before jumping into the back of Gabe's car.

"Good evening, Miss Stanz."

"Hey Gabe."

He looks at me in the mirror as he pulls out of the parking lot. He jumps onto the parkway and drives west, towards the city. He gives me the rundown. "Same guy as last week. I'll be overseeing your meal. Don't get returned again and you should be off her shit list, for a while anyway."

I slip my bracelet around my ankle and then lean back in the seat. "I'm always on her shit list."

"That's a bad place to be."

"Can I ask you something?" Gabe grunts and looks at me in the mirror. "How long do girls do this? I mean, how many clients do they see before they quit?"

He shakes his head. "Most get fired. There are a few that are really good at what they do. They create addicts. That's what Black wants. Guys that are so addicted to your kind of sex that they'll pay anything to get it. So getting returned kind of screws that up."

"That guy was a dick." I look out the window as I say it. I'm still mad at Sean about that, but I'd rather be on my way to see him than Henry.

"Obviously, but that's unheard of. Lure this new guy into a third contract and all will be forgiven. After that, it's anyone's guess how long you'll last. "

The rest of the ride passes in silence. My heart is lurching like I have to get a root canal in the middle of the mall or something equally horrific. I liked Henry. He was sweet. I need to get my head in the game or I'm going to screw this up.

CHAPTER 12

By the time that we pull up at the restaurant, I feel more poised. Gabe pulls up to the curb and the valet opens the door. I step from the back of the car, smooth my sexy, red, silk dress and look up.

Henry is standing a few feet away. He waves at me and hurries over. "You look stunning."

I smile warmly at him and take his arm when he offers it. "So do you." My voice is a little too deep, but that's okay. It's better to think I'm a sex fiend, right? We walk inside and get led to a table at the back of the restaurant. It's an Italian place with stucco walls and a rich red carpet that matches the color of my dress. Each table has a drippy candle in the center, along with beautiful plates and a million pieces of silverware.

When we are both seated, Henry orders wine. I smile at him from under my lashes. I decided to take Mel's advice and pretend this is a date. "So, how has your day been?"

He beams at me. "Fantastic. I can't even begin to tell you what that patent has done for me. I wanted to see you again. I had to thank you."

"You could have done that without all this." I wink at him and the man smiles harder. Damn, he's cute. He's acting like I'm a goddess or something. Every compliment lights him up to full wattage.

"Yes, but I wanted the chance to show you off and tell everyone I meet that you're the woman who changed my life. You tamed the beast for me. Ferro had no intention of giving me that patent, but you got it from him. It makes me wonder what you're capable of, so I wanted to take you out, alone, to see for myself." His gaze is dark. Henry's eyes don't dip below my neckline even though I'm sure he can see the little bumps from the crystals under my dress. He doesn't look.

Sean stares. *Stop thinking about Sean.*

I lean forward and say in a breathy voice, "You will."

The meal passes quickly. I try not to think about later, about doing things with him afterward, but images of naked bodies flash through my mind and sour my stomach. After dessert, I excuse myself. As I pass by the bar, Gabe falls into step with me.

"One hundred and ten percent, Stanz. I've already told her that the guy is eating out of your hand."

"Thanks, Gabe."

He nods and turns like he was going somewhere else. When I'm in the bathroom, I walk up in front of the sink and stare at the mirror. I want to splash water on my face, but it'll mess up make-up. I stand there for a moment and primp until I'm alone. Then, I sigh and try to work up the nerve to do whatever I need to do with Henry. I'm not cut out for this. Sex and love are tied together in my brain. I don't know how to tear them apart.

That's why you can't be with Sean. That's why you can't finish your job tonight.

I look at myself. This isn't what I thought my life would be like. But the money, oh my God, the money is good. Does it really matter that I fucked a really nice guy to survive? I might have slept with Henry anyway. He's sweet and funny and… not Sean.

When I leave the ladies room, I know what I need to do. I plaster a sexy smile on my face and saunter back to the table where Henry is waiting for me.

"Are you ready to go?" Henry stands and offers his hand.

I take it in mine. I lean in close to him and run my fingers over his shirt front, letting my fingers slip between the buttons. "I can't wait."

Henry squeezes my hand and we head out to the car. He remains a gentleman all the way up to the hotel room. He doesn't try to kiss me or do more than hold my hand. He smiles like he's happy to be with me and holding hands in enough. But I'm not that naïve. I said I'd do anything he wanted once we were in the hotel room. For all I know, he might be as twisted as Sean.

My heart pounds a little harder as Henry opens the door. I brush past him slowly, making sure I'm a tad too close. My chest brushes against his. I smile as I do it. Henry sucks in a jagged breath, and steps inside, letting the door close behind him.

He finally looks at my cleavage and his eyes wander over my smooth satin dress to the bumps where the silver rings are located. "Are your nipples pierced, Miss Stanz?" A surprised smile lines his lips.

"Sort of, Mr. Thomas. You'll have to wait and see for yourself." Henry knows me as Allison Stanz. Half of the time I don't respond fast enough when he says Allison. I need to act like I want this. I need this job, I need Henry to want me so badly that he's willing to triple his payment to have me a third time, assuming I get through this tonight.

Henry makes a content sound in the back of his throat and steps towards me. He hesitates for a second and then dips his head and presses his lips to mine. I lift my hands and tangle them in his hair, but he breaks the kiss before it gets going.

Holding out his arm, he says, "There are some things I want to know about you first."

I'm knocked off balance, but try to hide it. I smile at him and sit down in a chair. Henry sits next to me. His eyes are on his hand, which he places on my thigh.

I touch my hand to his and say, "It's all right. I'm yours. You can do anything you want."

Henry presses his lips together and looks up at me. "That's just it. You're not mine, Allison. This is an illusion; I'm not naïve enough to think it isn't. For all I know, you're not even into guys like me, but the thing is, I'm really into you. I wish I could ask you on a date. I wish I knew you, the real you, and not this version." He laughs and pulls his hand away. He stands and walks over to the bar. Pouring a glass of Jack, he turns back to me and says, "I'm a fool. I've paid an exorbitant amount of money for a beautiful woman who will do anything I want, and I say things like that."

I stand and walk up behind him. I touch his shoulder lightly. "Is that why you're being so careful? Are you afraid I won't like you?" I turn him toward me and take the Jack out of his hand and put it on the dresser behind him.

"Here's the truth," I manage to spin a web of lies that sounds so convincing even I believe it. I have to believe it or I won't be able to be with him. "I think you're incredibly sexy. The moment I saw you, I wanted to wrap my arms around your chest. And, the way you acted at dinner the other night was incredible. I am attracted to you. I would have gone on a date with you, and this *did* feel like a date. A really good date." I slip my arms around his neck and press my breasts against his chest. "It's up to you how it ends."

My heart is pounding. I want this and I don't want this. Henry is older than me with a runner's lean body. He's all hard muscle. I can see that, but he doesn't turn me on. There's no spark.

We stand still for a moment. Henry looks down at me and sighs. "Is this the only way to have you?"

I smile slowly. "For now."

"It's cruel to give me hope, Allison, but I'll take what I can get."

I nod. I'm Allison. I keep forgetting that.

Henry dips his head and kisses me. My hands find the sides of his face as I kiss him back. I close my eyes and picture Sean. When Henry's hands slide down my sides and cup my butt, I think of Sean's strong hands holding me tight. I moan a little and lean into him more, but Henry kisses me slowly, gently. He's lingering, so I follow his lead and slow down. The kiss dawdles and then Henry finally dips his head and kisses my neck. I tilt my head back and think about Sean kissing me in the dressing room. My body is confused. It remembers Sean's kisses, but it knows this isn't Sean.

Henry lifts his head and whispers in my ear, "Come to bed with me."

He pulls my hand across the room to the bed and sits down and scoots back to the middle. I crawl toward him in my tight dress. His eyes dip to my neckline and stay there. As I crawl toward him, I slip up his body, brushing my chest against him.

Henry closes his eyes for a moment. When I lick my tongue across the seam of his lips, he looks up at me. He takes me in his arms and kisses me harder this time. I fall onto his chest, which makes the silver clips bite into me. It sends a jolt between my legs and I moan into his mouth. Henry kisses me until he's breathless. Then, he flips me over and trails kisses down my neck and to my chest. He stops and traces his finger over the top of my breast. It's sweet, almost hesitant.

"You can touch me, Henry." I sit up and unzip my dress. I push the top down so he can see the bra.

"Oh, God." Henry sucks in air like there isn't enough. He stares at my breasts, salivating. I know he wants to touch, but he doesn't. He just looks at me and freezes. His eyes rise to my face. "How far would you go on a second date?"

I don't understand his question. I smile at him. "It depends on the guy. With you, second base is a given, and if you keep looking at me like that I might not be able to control myself."

The words feel like acid in my mouth. I hate lying. I imagine what I'd say to Sean if he asked me that. I shouldn't feel any remorse. Sean is fucking some other call girl right now, but I don't enjoy this. I put on the best sexy smile I can manage and crawl toward him on my hands and knees with my dress pushed down around my waist. "Kiss me, Henry. Don't make me beg for it."

Henry takes me in his arms and kisses me forever. I lose track of time, but it feels like he's avoiding doing anything more. When I reach for his belt, Henry shifts so he's on top of me. He finally dips his head to my breast. His lips are gentle.

I close my eyes and imagine I'm somewhere else. I want this to be over. My heart pounds harder and I realize that I'm afraid. Henry's lips press against me over and over, but they feel like razor wire. There's no connection, no desire. I know I need to force it. I thought lust would override my brain at some point, but it isn't happening.

Henry's hands move up and down my body and he pulls me up onto his lap. He dips his head and sucks my taut nipples between his lips. I finally respond. His touch, and the ring clamped around me, makes it so I'd have to be numb not to. My hips buck into his and I tilt my head back. I grab hold of that feeling, knowing I need to hold onto it to do this. I keep picturing Sean and begin to feel more into it. My hands tangle in his hair and I say things, but I don't hear the words. Henry stays there like that, kissing my breasts, neck, and lips until he suddenly stops. Henry pushes away and shakes his head.

I'm flushed and breathing hard. I don't understand why he got up. "What's wrong?"

He rubs his hands over his head and down his neck. "Nothing. Nothing at all. You're perfect."

"Then, why'd you get up?"

He smiles at me, still trying to catch his breath. "You said second base. I have to stop or I won't be able to."

I grin at him and get up. His eyes fixate on my bra. The crystals are still dangling from my nipples. He finally tears his gaze away and looks up at my face. "You don't have to stop, Henry. It's okay, really." I slip my arms around his neck and lock my eyes with his.

He shakes his head. "It's my fantasy, Allison. I want it to play out longer."

I don't know what to do. Is he returning me? I freak out a little bit, but try not to show it. "So what do you want to do now? It's still early."

Henry steps back and pushes me away. "Please, put your dress on. I'll arrange another date with you. We can hit third base next time."

I smile at him, and reach forward, gently touching his arm. "Henry, I'm yours now." He looks over at me with lust in his eyes, but he's torn. I can see it all over his face. He wants me in a way that he can't have me. "Have you hired a call girl before?"

"Not for this." He watches me for a moment, and then lowers his lashes.

I wrap my arms around him and hold on tight. I hug him because he's the sweetest man alive. I kiss his cheek and then step back and pull up my straps and zip my dress. "I can imagine why. You seriously bought me so you could date me?"

He nods. "It's the only way, right?" I nod. His eyes drift over my dress.

An idea crosses my mind. I wonder if I should press him, but I do it anyway. I unzip my dress again and start to pull it down. "I want to show you something."

He waves his hands at me. "That's unnecessary." He actually looks away like he shouldn't be watching me, but he can't help it. Henry keeps peeking at me out of the corner of his eye.

"Oh, it's totally necessary. I want to show you what you missed." I drop the dress to the floor and stand there in my little nothing bottoms and walk slowly toward him. "Do you still want to wait until next time?"

Henry swallows hard. His eyes sweep over me. "You're not playing fair."

I smile at him and back up. I want to make sure he asks for me again. This dating thing could help secure my job. I give him a sexy smile. "No, I'm not. Pick up your phone and take my picture. I want you to look at it later when I'm gone."

Henry grabs his phone off the counter and takes a few quick pictures of me. I lay on the bed and he snaps more. When he's done, I take it and delete all but one shot. Henry looks down at his one picture. "That was evil."

"Allison does evil things." I grin at him and slip my dress back on.

"Yes, you do." After I'm dressed, he comes over and pulls me against him again. Henry presses his lips to mine and kisses me again. When he's breathless, he pulls away. "You better go."

He walks me to the door. I lean in and brush my lips lightly to his. "Good night, Henry. I can't wait to see you again." I wink at him and turn away. I make sure to sway my hips as I walk away. I can feel his eyes on me. I hope I made the right decision. I didn't want to push him. It felt like he'd regret it. Henry wants this to feel real, so I'll make it real.

When I walk outside, I see Gabe smoking at the edge of the sidewalk. I shift around people, cut through the crowds on the sidewalk, and make my way over to him.

Gabe shakes his head. "Did you get thrown out?"

"Nope. I think I did good. I wanted to tell you that I'm done for the night. I'm going to hang out in the city for a while. I'll check in tomorrow. Have a good night." I'm smiling too much. I can't wait to see Sean.

Before I turn to walk away, Gabe nods. His voice follows after me. "You want me to drop you off?"

I turn back. "No, that's okay."

Gabe stands and takes a long pull on the cigarette before putting it out. As he walks over to me, he lets out the smoke. "I know where you're going. Let me drive you so you don't get mugged on the way there. You can't go in the subway looking like that." Gabe shakes his head, like I have no brains.

I'm not dumb enough to deny anything. "Will you tell her?"

"Only if I'm asked, Miss Stanz, and since I already know you're screwing Mr.

Ferro, I think it's safer if I drive you to his hotel."

"I'm not screwing him!"

He gives me a look. "Call it what you want, but it'll get you fired. Wait here. I'll get the limo."

Gabe returns to the curb with the car moments later, and then drives me a few blocks to Sean's hotel. I'm early and really excited. I thought I'd be creeped out and covered in sweat. Instead, I feel pretty good.

Before we pull up, Gabe says, "Something's wrong with him, you know. More so than with other guys. Ferro did something."

I lean forward. "What are you talking about?"

Gabe is in line to get to the drop-off. He pulls the car up. We're next. "It was in the papers a few years back. Plus the guy is *off*. Don't trust him. I know you do, I can see it on your face, but you're not an old guy like me. I see what he is. I wish you'd stop this. The guy you were just with is safer than Ferro."

"What are you talking about? What did Sean do?" I finish my question just as we pull up. The hotel worker opens the door. I hesitate. I want to hear what Gabe has to say, but he's silent.

I step out of the car and watch him pull away. The floor of my stomach twists and the skin on my neck prickles. I look up at the building. The windows are lit all the way up to the penthouse. I go inside and try to shake off the bad vibe that's crawling over my skin.

The elevator carries me up and I'm on Sean's floor. Smiling, I walk towards his room just as the door opens. I stop in my tracks when I see who steps out. I hear her voice, and see her, but I can't believe it. Part of my brain keeps telling me that she wouldn't do that to me, but there she is. A million emotions collide until I can't think.

Mel. It's Mel. She said she was working tonight. She's the only other girl at Black's that will do the things Sean wants. She mentioned a sick guy a few weeks ago. Now I know who she meant.

Sean stands in the doorway with his shirt unbuttoned, holding the door open.

His dark hair is tousled and his cheeks are rosy. Images of him and Mel together flash through my mind. I want to scream. I want to walk over there and shriek at both of them, but I don't move. I'm frozen.

I wish I could rewind and start over. I wish I never met him. In a matter of seconds, I've lost my best friend and Sean. It's as if he feels my eyes on his face. Sean slowly looks up and freezes. Our eyes lock. His lips part and everything seems to happen in slow motion. Mel turns and has the same horrified expression on her face.

Before either of them says anything, I step towards Mel. "How could you!" My hand flies and I slap her in the face. My palm stings as she closes her eyes and takes the hit. Mel doesn't move.

I glance at Sean, but I can't even speak. My fists clench and unclench at my sides. I breathe too hard and feel my throat tighten. Tears sting my eyes as betrayal snakes its way into my heart.

I turn on my heel and run.

THE ARRANGEMENT SERIES

This story unfolds over the course of multiple short novels. Each one follows the continuing story of Avery Stanz and Sean Ferro.

To ensure you don't miss the next installment, text **AWESOMEBOOKS** to **22828** and you will get an email reminder on release day.

MORE ROMANCE BOOKS BY
H.M. WARD

DAMAGED

DAMAGED 2

SCANDALOUS

SCANDALOUS 2

STRIPPED

SECRETS

THE SECRET LIFE OF TRYSTAN
SCOTT

And more.
To see a full book list, please visit:

www.SexyAwesomeBooks.com